艾菲的天使

ALFIE'S ANGELS

Henritta Barkow

Sarah Garson

Chinese translation by Sylvia Denham

mantra

艾菲想做天使。

他在書中見過他們，

Alfie wanted to be an angel.
He'd seen them in his books.

他在夢中見過他們。

He'd seen them in his dreams.

Angels have wings and angels can fly.
Alfie wanted wings so he could fly to
school on time.

天使有翅膀，天使可以飛。

艾菲想有翅膀，好讓他能準時飛到學校上學。

天使可以跳舞，天使可以用甜美的歌聲唱歌。
艾菲想唱歌，好讓他能參加合唱團。

Angels can dance, and sing in beautiful voices.
Alfie wanted to sing so that he could be in the choir.

天使走動快速敏捷。

Angels can move faster than the eye can see.

艾菲想快速走動，
好讓他能射入更多的球。

Alfie wanted to move faster so
that he could score more goals.

天使有各種形狀 ...

Angels come in all shapes...

... 和大小，

...and sizes,

他們更能做最神奇驚異的事。

and they can do the most amazing things.

艾菲想做天使。

Alfie wanted to be an angel.

他在書中見過他們，

他在夢中見過他們。

He'd seen them in his books.
He'd seen them in his dreams.

孩子每年都有一次可以成爲天使，
老師挑選他們，家長打扮他們，
全學校都觀看他們。

Now once a year children can be angels.
The teachers choose them.
The parents dress them.
The whole school watches them.

艾菲的老師總是挑選女孩子，

Alfie's teacher always chose the girls.

最漂亮的女孩子，頭髮最長的女孩子，
有最大的眼睛和最甜美的笑容的女孩子。

The prettiest girls. The girls with the longest hair.
The girls with the biggest eyes and the sweetest smiles.

但艾菲想做天使。

他在書中見過他們，

他在夢中見過他們。

But Alfie wanted to be an angel.
He'd seen them in his books.
He'd seen them in his dreams.

當老師問：「誰想做天使？」
艾菲舉手。

When the teacher asked, "Who wants to be an angel?"Alfie put up his hand.

女同學大笑，男同學竊笑，

The girls laughed. The boys sniggered.

老師盯著他，想一下說道「艾菲想做天使？但只有女孩子做天使的啊。」

The teacher stared. The teacher thought and said, "Alfie wants to be an angel? But only girls are angels."

艾菲慢慢地搖頭，

他告訴老師他所知有關天使的一切，

Alfie slowly shook his head,
and he told his teacher all about the angels.

他如何在書中見過他們，

他如何在夢中見過他們。

How he'd seen them in his books.
How he'd seen them in his dreams.

艾菲一面說，他全班的同學一面聽。

And the more Alfie spoke,
the more the whole class listened.

沒有人因爲艾菲想做天使而大笑，

也沒有人竊笑。

Nobody laughed and nobody sniggered,
because Alfie wanted to be an angel.

現在又是每年讓小孩子做一次天使的時候，
老師指導他們，家長打扮他們，
全學校都觀看他們載歌載舞。

Now it was that time of year when children could be angels. The teachers taught them. The parents dressed them. The whole school watched them while they sang and danced.

艾菲終於是天使了。

Alfie was an angel!